DELIVER ME FROM EVIL

ADELAIDE FORREST

Cover design by: Adelaide Forrest
Proofreading by: Light Hand Proofreading

Printed in the United States of America

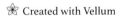 Created with Vellum

DISCLAIMER

Deliver Me from Evil features an Alpha male who claims his woman quickly. If insta-love romance isn't your thing, turn back now. This fast and dirty read is the perfect quick escape into total and instant devotion.

1

DELIVERANCE

*D*irt and grime washed down the drain, staining the sink basin with the mud of the Earth. The space under my fingernails never quite came clean. It served as a constant reminder of the hard life I lived in service to our leader. I did the best I could, stepping out of the bathroom to find my mother waiting for me. She'd never pulled me from my duty midday before, and the nagging sensation that something was wrong slithered up my spine. "Come sit," she said, a soft smile transforming her tired face. Holding out a hand, she took mine and inspected it with dissatisfaction. Frowning briefly at the callouses covering my palm and fingertips, she forced another smile to her face and gestured me to the chair.

She rarely doted on me. It just wasn't our way. Devotion to God, Jonathan, and the *Children of Awe* came first and foremost. Parenting was a duty — not an act of love. Nothing but a means to an end to produce more of the Disciples who could serve our community.

I averted my eyes to the floor as I sat in her favored chair in front of the sole mirror in our home. It was where she prepared herself daily to my father's exact expectations, a right only afforded to the married women amongst us according to the tenets of our community. One wasn't to look upon oneself with vanity. The only purpose of beauty was to make it easier for our husbands to fulfill their duty, and to tempt nature by flaunting such a thing for other men to see was the work of the Devil. Such rules had been ingrained in me since I was a child, and I'd never disobeyed. Never so much as glanced at my reflection in the mirror.

It didn't matter what I looked like if I was a good, pious girl. I wanted a kind husband, and the best way to achieve that was to be known for exemplary behavior.

My eyes remained on the floor as Mother brushed my long and straight, deep brown hair down my back. "There are rumors that today Jonathan will announce his decision to take a new First Wife." My body froze, and she ignored my stillness. The First Wife to Jonathan was responsible for childbearing, for providing his heirs. She was the one who shared his bed and sat beside him at meals, while the others served him in different ways. As she pulled my hair into sections, I thought for a moment she might braid it for me. I'd been left to do it myself for so long that under any other circumstances, the feel of her delicate fingers working through my hair might have thawed the ice in my veins. Instead, she pulled one side to the front of my shoulder, fluffing it gently and setting the brush down on the vanity. Her other hand moved under my chin, those fingers tickling the sensitive flesh where I'd not been touched for years. Without the love of a mother or father who saw me as anything but their responsibility, I rarely knew the comfort of another person's touch.

She lifted my chin gently, a passive signal for me to look up. Still, I couldn't bring myself to. Not when I knew what it would mean if she wanted me to look in the mirror. "But he already has two," I protested. My lungs burned with the need to breathe, but there was no escaping the crushing weight on my chest. Jonathan had only just married Noelle three years prior. He would do as he pleased with no one to stop him, but after all the commotion he caused in his assertion that Noelle was chosen by God, I couldn't imagine him setting her aside so quickly. To so blatantly diminish everything he'd put the community through with his determination.

"Emily is too old to give him any more children," my mother chastised. "And he needs a son to inherit his legacy and bring the next generation to heel in the eyes of God."

"What of Noelle? She is only twenty." Panic rose in me as those slender and delicate fingers lifted harder, but still I chose to ignore them. Tucking my chin tighter despite her growing pressure.

"And she has failed to fall pregnant even once in those three years. No, it would seem God does not intend for her to be mother to our next leader. God has a plan for all things, but not every one of us can live to the full potential He sees for us."

I swallowed hard. "You think he will choose Adela?"

"Absolutely not. She may be the greatest beauty we have, but she is obstinate and only 15. After the attention marrying Noelle at seventeen brought, I do not believe Jonathan will want to put his Disciples through that again." As soon as outsiders had got wind of a fifty-year-old church leader marrying a 17-year-old, reporters had become fascinated with our community and invaded the privacy we thrived in.

"Then who?" I asked.

"I think he will choose you." I clenched my eyes tight,

shuddering at the thought. "Deliverance," she hissed, yanking my head up so sharply I couldn't resist. My closed eyes were the only things that kept me from seeing my face clearly for the first time. When I'd been young, the other girls and I made a game of trying to draw one another, of looking at reflective surfaces of water, to try to see ourselves. Even with my limited experience, it seemed a strange sensation not to know what others saw when they looked at you, but it was all we were allowed to know until chosen to wed. "It is an honor to be chosen to wed at all, let alone to our leader himself."

"He's so old, Mama."

"He is wise. He serves God, and if he chooses you to marry him, you will do your duty with a smile, because it means you will serve God through him."

I wrung my hands together, picking at the dirty callouses surrounding my nails. "Has he set Noelle aside already?"

Mother nodded. "Victoria saw him moving her things into one of the spare bedrooms." Which didn't mean he wouldn't still bed her, even after he took a new wife. There was no divorce within the *Children of Awe*. She helped me stand, giving a cursory glance down to the dirt-stained hem of my white floor-length dress as I opened my eyes and looked to my feet.

With a disapproving tut, she pulled one of her own out of her closet and tugged the one I wore over my head. Hers was a lighter fabric, more luxurious than the ones I usually wore to the garden. The elbow-length sleeves hung off my arms loosely, but the vee at my chest flattered the cut that was fitted through my waist before it flared out at my hips. "You will not disappoint me," she chided, pressing on my shoulders until I dropped back into the chair.

"Yes, Mama," I murmured, and I didn't fight it when she

grabbed the hair at the back of my head and used her grip to tilt my head up to the mirror. I knew very well my mother would not encourage me to look upon myself if she didn't believe with all her heart that Jonathan would choose me that day.

My hair, while sleek, was thick and healthy as it fell over my breast covered by the thin dress. My grey eyes were rounded with shock, and my skin was tanned from all the time I spent in the gardens, toiling away under the scorching summer sun to prepare for the colder months. Freckles spotted my skin as Mama patted my cheek softly. "You see? You will make Jonathan very happy, my daughter."

I swallowed, letting her pull me to stand. Even if it felt more like walking to my funeral than potentially my wedding. I'd only wanted to be happy with a husband who loved me.

Never this.

∞∞∞

My stomach thumped with each pulse of my heart, the skin and muscles spasming so hard that I felt it throughout my body. My father led me up the Sanctuary aisle, directly plotting the steps one woman would take soon enough, if my mother's rumors were true.

I wanted them to be a lie, but the joyous faces of the genuinely devout girls squashed whatever ray of hope I'd clung to. Dropping me with the other unwed daughters, my father took his place next to Jonathan.

They'd been friends since their childhood in the town at the base of the mountain. And when Jonathan came to the woods to start his community, my father took my mother and followed him. He would follow Jonathan wherever he led.

One girl beside me grabbed my hand in solidarity. One of the few who sometimes joined me in the gardens after curfew to feel free for just a few moments. I knew she, too, longed to experience the mysterious concept of choice.

Like me, all she wanted was the right to choose.

Jonathan stepped forward from the small group of his most loyal, and the moment he turned his eyes on the crowd of his followers, we dropped to our knees on the Church floor. Bowing my head in submission, I set my hands on my thighs and waited for his voice to ring out in the cavernous space. The Church and Jonathan's home were the only opulent possessions we had as a community. Admittedly, that was part of the reason many girls sought to become one of his wives. Why they didn't mind knowing that they wouldn't be the only ones to serve their husband.

"Rise my children. Let this be a day of celebration, and not of mourning. For even in the most bittersweet of God's news, we can find the light."

"Amen," we agreed, rising to our feet gracefully. With plenty of practice, even the most uncoordinated among us did it fluidly.

"It is with great sadness, but also great joy, that I inform you God has decided it is time for me to choose another wife from our flock!" The Disciples cheered at his proclamation, not bothering to consider what it might mean for the two wives he'd set aside already. To be deemed barren was unthinkable in a community where women's primary purpose was to provide and raise children. "It would appear Noelle has proven unable to meet the promise God saw in her when he chose her for me." At his side, tears streamed down Noelle's face, but she remained silent with her head bowed in submission. Her embarrassment was palpable in the air, and my heart beat in sympathy for her. "I believe His next choice will be everything he hopes and more. I believe she will deliver us a bounty of heirs to lead us into the next generation!"

Oh God.

"Deliverance, would you join me please, my dear girl?" he asked, and I gasped as the people around me echoed praises for the decision. I was well-liked in my community, always following the commandments and pleasing my parents. But with the naturally competitive way the Disciples sought approval, I never could have expected I would have much support from the others.

I owed any kindness I received to my father's status. I walked to the front, my quivering upper lip the only sign that betrayed that I felt myself shattering. "God has chosen you for me," Jonathon whispered as I bent and obediently pressed my forehead to his extended hand. "What say you?" The question gave me the illusion of choice, but there was none. Not really.

"God honors me," I whispered with fake reverence. He pulled his hand back, giving me the signal it was acceptable to stand straight. His fingers at my chin tilted my gaze to his.

"My beautiful bride," he murmured to me. We will wed on the morrow," he announced to the crowd, and his eyes took the hungry glint I'd grown used to seeing on the faces of men just before they took their new brides to bed.

I swallowed, casting my eyes to my mother briefly. The stern look that met my hesitation reaffirmed everything I already knew. I'd have no support if I chose not to follow the path chosen for me.

I'd wed Jonathan, or I would leave the only home I'd ever known.

2

DELIVERANCE

*R*unning.

    I had to keep running, even though my body felt ready to give out. I pushed it even further. Dusk had barely fallen when Jonathan announced us married in the eyes of God and took my hand to bring me back to his home.

Our home.

I shivered, although my body was drenched in sweat. I'd long since run out of tears. The dehydration of my body proved too much to produce any more.

Night had long since fallen, the moon shining down through the trees from its place high in the sky, signaling just how long I'd run for my life. Perhaps Jonathan wouldn't kill me, but he'd made it very clear what he would do if I didn't serve him as a wife should. I'd thought I could. Thought myself capable of just closing my eyes and waiting for it to be over.

I wasn't.

I tripped, catching my bare foot on a tree root. I controlled my shriek as best I could as I collided with the

Earth, smacking my head against the ground hard enough to daze myself. Whimpering, I tried to push back up to my feet, but exhaustion dragged me back to the ground. I felt the hard crust of blood coating my thigh, my fat and swollen lip, and the sharp ache in my wrist that I cradled to my chest protectively. Everything hurt.

My *soul* hurt.

I'd always suspected there was something off about our too-charming leader, but I'd never suspected this. I'd never expected a monster.

And my parents willingly gave me to him.

"Please," I beseeched when I tried and failed to push myself to my feet one more time. My throat ached around the word, desperate for the water I'd deprived it, for hours now of exertion. With another whimper, I used my good arm to drag myself against the trunk of the tree for cover. Lost in the woods as I was, nobody heard my plea. Civilization was miles away at the base of the mountain, so with a tearless sob I did the only thing I could do.

I curled into a ball and retreated into sleep, knowing the greatest mercy God could give me would be to die before I woke. To never suffer the cruel touch of my husband again.

" ucking shit," I cursed, kicking the frame of the raised garden. I'd come a long way in the five years since I'd moved up Mount Awe, but the one thing I never seemed to get any better at was gardening. Midsummer had already arrived, and with it the first lackluster growth of vegetables in my garden. I hated going into the city unless I absolutely had to, and a shortage of vegetables from the garden would mean another trip this fall. Coleman thought I was dumb for dreading those supply runs, since they were the only opportunity we had to socialize and meet women. But the empty, casual encounters that came from a single night in town hadn't been enough for me in years.

Maybe even longer, if I was honest with myself.

I didn't want a woman invading my space and most women weren't made for the hard life I lived. I'd never met one who would be content without WiFi. One who would love simply reading a book by the fire after sunset.

Maybe it wasn't so much as I didn't want a woman in my space, but more that, with every passing season I became more and more convinced the woman I dreamed of didn't exist.

The solar lights flickered over my head briefly, and I wiped the dirt from my hands onto my jeans in frustration. I turned my back on the gardens, going back to the main cabin and snatching my rifle from the mudroom.

I may not be able to grow my own damn food for shit, but I could hunt. There'd been a time in my life when my ability to kill was the only thing keeping me from a hole in the ground. I moved to the edge of the property slowly, giving my eyes time to adjust to the darkness that surrounded me. While I always carried a flashlight in my pocket, the light would only alert the animal life to my presence.

Even though I didn't normally hunt quite this early in the morning, it was always dark when I headed out. I hadn't gone to bed the night before, because, while I didn't normally have trouble sleeping, something kept me up. Twisting and turning in my bed felt less and less comfortable with every hour that passed, until I had no choice but to get up and be productive despite the dark hour.

Life mostly off the grid meant there was always something to be done. Always some chore demanding my attention. It was too much for one man, and there was no alternative aside living with my buddy, Coleman.

And living with Coleman would drive me insane within twenty-four hours.

I moved through the woods silently, lifting my feet high to avoid tripping on the shadowed forest floor, as I kept my eyes peeled for deer poking their heads out for the first time that day. A scuff sounded behind me, making me spin in place quickly and raise my gun. Squinting through the pre-dawn, I tried to find whatever had made the noise.

I sighed when I found a hare sniffing at the base of a tree, but the long strands it stood on didn't belong. Pulling the flashlight from my pocket, I shone it on the area. The hare hurried off, disappearing into the distance while my entire world narrowed to the sight of a body on the ground. Dark hair shielded her face and her curled up body. The white dress she wore was torn, ragged, and dirty. Glancing around, I stepped closer cautiously, waiting for her to move.

I gently nudged her shoulder with my boot, watching in growing rage as she flipped to her back easily, without resistance, like there was nothing left in her to fight. Blood stained the front of her white dress, her skin covered in goosebumps where it was left bare. Her bottom lip was split, the skin surrounding it bruised. With her eyes closed, she looked like a battered angel. Slinging my rifle over my shoulder, I knelt at her side and reached out a hand to touch her cheek, feeling satisfied when her eyelashes fluttered slightly.

She was alive.

She whimpered, moving her arm tighter to her chest in her slumber, and it was in that moment that I saw the deep purple fingerprints on her skin. The odd angle of her wrist. I shoved my flashlight into my pocket, then, standing once again, I leaned over and pulled her into my arms as gently as I could. She gave another whimper, tucking her face tighter into my shoulder as she let out a ragged breath.

"Shhh," I soothed, taking extra care not to trip on my journey home. I couldn't afford to fall with her in my arms. "You're safe now."

I didn't even know her name, but I already knew I'd never let anything hurt her again.

J woke to a throbbing in my head and an ache all over, but the surface I lay on was soft and warm. Unfamiliarly so. I remembered my wrist injury only after trying to push to a sitting position with it. Crying out, I whimpered as I cradled it in my good hand. The moment my eyes landed on the water bottle sitting on the nightstand, I snatched it up and swallowed the liquid greedily.

"You're awake," a deep voice murmured from the doorway to the room. I sat up quickly, using my left arm, and clutched the blankets to my chest. "We should get you cleaned up and fed." The gruff and rugged tenor of his voice suited him. Over six feet of tall, bulky muscle wrapped in a tee-shirt and athletic shorts. He seemed enormous compared to the slighter men of the compound; more masculine, he made them look like boys.

With his hazel eyes intense on me, even from across the room, I flinched back. Pressing into the wooden headboard, I stared at him with a trembling lip. "I won't hurt you, Baby," he tried to assure me, but my attention darted around the room. The clearly masculine bedroom with his clothes exploding from the dresser and an overflowing laundry basket in the corner.

"Where am I?" I asked, eyeing him warily as he took a step toward me.

"My home," he returned, approaching and sitting at the foot of the bed, keeping some distance for my comfort. There was no malice in his eyes or harshness to his features. I'd seen true evil on my husband's face before he struck, for that fleeting moment before fear blinded me. "I found you unconscious in the woods and brought you back here."

Reality crashed in and I glanced around for a clock, but there was none in the room. "I have to go." Throwing the blankets off me, I stood on wobbly feet that stung with blisters and cuts from my moonlit run through the woods. Glancing down, it comforted me to see that my feet were still caked in mud. That my dress was torn and filthy, and the same one I'd fled the compound in.

"No," he said simply, standing and crossing his arms over his chest. "I'm not about to let you run through the woods. Especially not in your condition. We're going to get you cleaned up, in fresh clothes, and then you're going to tell me all about your troubles while I make you some lunch."

"Lunch?" I asked, casting a glance at the windows. It *was* quite sunny.

He tilted his head curiously. "You slept damn near two days. You woke up once enough to use the bathroom, but not enough to remember."

My voice came out as a whimper, and I glanced back at the door. "No," I gasped. How long could I expect to evade Jonathan and the Disciples when I'd lost my head start?

"You're safe here," he reiterated, seeming to follow the path of my thoughts.

"They'll find me. I didn't make it far enough," I whispered. "I don't want to go back."

"And I repeat, you're safe here. Nobody is going to hurt you on my watch." He took a step to the side, positioning himself more directly between me and the door and blocking my only escape.

I shook my head. "I can't ask you to—"

"You didn't. I'm telling you I will protect you. I do not take kindly to hurt women running themselves dead tired through these woods. Teaching whoever did this a lesson will be a pleasure." He paused, studying me when I didn't make another move for the door. "Why don't we start with your name?"

I hesitated. Jonathan hammered it into our heads that outsiders hated the Disciples. That they didn't understand our purpose and our commitment to God. Would he throw me out when he knew the truth?

Despite my desire to run only moments before, something about having him look at me differently didn't sit well with me. "Deliverance," I mumbled, watching his eyes go round with shock.

"You from that religious compound?" he whispered, his eyes narrowing on where I picked flakes of dirt off the fingers of my injured hand. Nodding back at him, I watched him through my lashes, waiting for his inevitable judgement. Jonathan's purpose had never been mine. My parent's beliefs had never been mine, but I'd been condemned to the life they chose for me, regardless.

A life in the world I knew existed outside our convent, compound, I guess, in the clearing in the woods, was impossible for me. I had no support network. No one to help me.

I couldn't even read.

"Right. My name is Anderson. You mind if I call you

Del?" he asked, making my head snap up to look at him fully.

I shook my head. A nickname meant he wouldn't kick me out just yet.

Didn't it?

"Bathroom is through that door. I'd leave you to it, but I highly suspect you're gonna need help again. Your wrist is fractured. I had a friend bring a splint by, and we'll get you set with that as soon as you get out of the shower."

He stepped into the room he'd said was the bathroom, running the water in the massive claw-foot tub. I watched through the open doorway, apprehension locking my feet to the spot. I couldn't force them to move, couldn't step into the bathroom with him.

Somehow, some way, I thought it might break me more if he hurt me the way Jonathan had tried to. To escape the clutches of one man only to run straight to another who would be cruel.

What was the point?

"I can handle it myself," I objected, keeping my voice kind. I'd never refused an order when they were given, never tried to defy my elders, and there was no question that he was older than me. Not nearly as old as Jonathan, but the faintest traces of wrinkles crinkled at the corners of his eyes when he smiled at me, in a way an eighteen-year-old boy's did not.

When I still didn't move, he crossed his arms over his chest and that smile faded into a smirk. "Is that so?"

I nodded hesitantly, finally making my way awkwardly into the bathroom. I kept my distance from him, clinging to the opposite wall of the small room. While the bedroom and bathroom weren't overly large, they were fitted with quality fixtures the likes of which I'd never seen. The compound had whatever we could get for free or cheap. His home was something he'd clearly put love into. Or maybe his wife had.

The thought bothered me more than it should.

"Let's see you get that dress off then," he challenged, holding his ground and watching me where I eyed the shower head.

"Could I have some privacy?" I asked, looking at the floor.

I drew in a ragged breath when he closed the distance between us. His fingers touched the sensitive skin underneath my chin, tipping my face until our eyes met. I couldn't breathe under the intensity of that piercing stare, but as his chest hovered only a breath from mine, I realized it never came for him either. His lungs never filled or expelled the air in him, as the moment hovered between us like something tangible was happening.

"Baby, there ain't no point to me leaving. We both know you got no shot of getting that dress off without my help." I glanced down at it, eying the torn hem with distaste. I'd have to bend in half just to reach the bottom, and the pain ripping through my torso made me wince at just the thought. "I promise I won't touch you in any way I don't absolutely need to, but let me help you." His voice was soft, and with a quiet sob I nodded as tears pool in my eyes. "Shh," he soothed, bunching the dress up my thighs and nudging me to lift my arms.

I swallowed and did, letting him carefully help me get my bad arm out of the fabric before he pulled it over my head. Wrapping my arms around my nude chest, I flushed all the way to my forehead. He kindly averted his eyes, checking the water temperature before he turned back to me. With a reassuring deep breath, he glanced down my body to where my underwear covered the most intimate part of me. His eyes caught on the blood encrusting the top of my thigh and the mark that could barely be seen beneath it. His body stilled in place with an eerie tension. I stood quietly, trying to make myself small and averting my gaze when his eyes blazed into mine. His jaw tensed as though he was biting something, and my eyes went all the way to his feet in submission.

"I'm sorry," I whispered.

"Don't you dare, Baby." His voice was soft, though laced with an edge of rage. His hands cupped my cheeks and startled me, drawing my gaze up to his. "I won't ever hurt you. I promise you that, but whoever did that to you? I'll kill him with my bare hands."

My fingers drifted down to touch the surface of my thigh, to the marks carved into my skin in the shape of a cross. I sniffled back my tears when I felt the crunch of clotted blood. "A mark for every disobedience," I whispered, thinking back to the callous words my husband spoke to me when I didn't want to fulfill my wifely duty on our wedding night. The vulgar words he'd spoken, the transformation in the man my parents followed happened as soon as we were safely closed inside the privacy of his home.

I didn't think most of the Disciples knew that the Devil lurked inside their leader, but my parents? I didn't know how my father could *not* know. Not with how long he'd been friends with Jonathan.

With his eyes still on the distinctive mark, he growled. "Is that one of their rules in the cult?"

I tilted my head in confusion, staring at him despite my discomfort with my nudity. He never looked away from my eyes as he waited for me to answer. "Cult?" I asked.

He sank his straight white teeth into his tense bottom

lip, seeming to consider his words. "That's what most people call that community. A cult is a group who have extreme religious beliefs that are strange to the rest of us. They usually follow a man. His word is law."

"God's word is law," I corrected automatically. "Jonathan is just his messenger." There was no judgement in Anderson's eyes as I thought over the words and the way they'd come so naturally. "I don't believe that," I admitted out loud, the first time I'd ever dared to voice my true thoughts. Jonathan was nothing but a man who took advantage of people who needed something to believe in so desperately that they clung to the illusion of faith he painted.

Sacrificing their daughters to his Tenets. Laboring while he enjoyed luxuries the rest of us could never dream to have.

"That's a good start." Anderson smiled, his fingers touching the edge of my underwear where they clung to my hips. He knelt at my feet, slowly and carefully peeling them down my legs. He took special care over the cross on my thigh, making sure not to let the fabric touch it. When he stood, he sighed and helped me step into the clawfoot tub. I let the hot water run over me, enjoyed the way it seared my skin and cleansed me of all the filth from my run through the woods. Anderson handed me a soapy cloth, and I used my good arm to scrub my skin clean. "I have to ask, even though I think I'll hate the answer. Did he rape you, Del?" I froze, glancing back over my shoulder at him.

The fact that I didn't understand one of his words, that it seemed like another language but wasn't, only highlighted just how isolated we were in our community. Education *he* didn't approve of didn't exist. "What is rape?"

He swallowed, clenching his fists at his side. "When a

man forces himself on you. Has sex with you without your permission."

I studied those rage-filled hazel eyes, somehow knowing that the only answer I could give would change everything. "He's my husband," I admitted in a whisper. "My body is his to do with as he pleases."

"Your body is yours and yours alone," Anderson growled, making me flinch back. "Nobody has the right to touch you without your permission."

I nodded my head, thinking the world outside the *Children of Awe* was far more different than I could have expected. "He didn't rape me. I'm still intact."

He stilled at my side, his mouth opening and closing briefly before he decided what to say. "But you said he is your husband?"

"We were married the day I ran. I couldn't go through with it. I didn't want him to touch me. He was furious, and he hit me." I touched my lip, feeling the scab where the flesh had split under the ring he always wore. "When I didn't concede immediately, he grabbed me and then marked me for the disobedience. I think he would have taken me to our marriage bed, but one of his other wives stepped in. She distracted him and told me to run away and never look back," I whispered, dropping my eyes to the floor in shame. "I left her."

"We'll help her. I'll send someone to help any who want to leave. I promise, Baby." He took the cloth from me when I finally finished scrubbing my body, tossing it into the sink on the other side of the room. Pulling the shower head off the hook, he encouraged me to tip my head back and used it to thoroughly wet my hair. The pressure felt like a heavenly massage, and for the first time I understood a bit of the pleasure my father must have felt when my mother rubbed his shoulders after he got home at night.

After he washed and rinsed my hair, I almost mourned the loss when he turned the water off, but the bliss of a soft towel wrapping around my body was enough to distract me from it. He disappeared into the bedroom, returning with a pair of underwear on top of a folded dress in a soft, golden fabric with little white flowers all over it. I reached out to touch the fabric slowly, the colors and pattern so striking compared to the bland whites I'd worn all my life.

"You like it?" he asked, and I turned my eyes up with a flush to my cheeks.

"It's beautiful."

"My buddy Coleman had a friend leave it at his place once. She won't miss it. We'll go into town to get you some new clothes once you've rested up." I resisted the urge to tell him I needed to get into town today. The conversation could wait until I wasn't naked. When I could just walk out the door when he wasn't paying attention.

A goodbye with him would hurt. Already, somehow, I knew leaving him would hurt more than leaving my entire community behind.

It was one more reason I needed to do it quickly. I couldn't bring my problems down on him. He helped me into the underwear and slipped the dress over my head, the fabric settling on my shoulders with only thin straps and stopping mid-thigh. I tugged at the lack of length, feeling inappropriate. I wore more fabric to sleep.

He turned, tugging open a drawer of the sink vanity and pulling out a tube of something. "Let me see that cut," he said, kneeling in front of me once again. With a nervous swallow, I lifted the dress slowly until the mark stood out like a beacon. Having been scrubbed clean, the angry red mark oozed blood slowly. Anderson dabbed it away with a new washcloth, applying the white cream from the tube to the wound. The touch of his rough fingers should have been a reminder of the pain, but instead an odd heat buzzed from my leg to my stomach. A big square bandage followed shortly after, and Anderson applied it to the area firmly before he nodded in satisfaction and stood.

"Let's get you fed," he announced, turning and striding for the bedroom. I settled the dress back down over the tops of my thighs, pulling at the lack of fabric again. He was oblivious to my plight, and I supposed beggars couldn't be choosers.

It would attract less attention than a torn and blood-stained dress.

∞∞∞

He made me a sandwich, piled high with some kind of thin-sliced meat and cheese and lettuce and tomato on the top. I devoured every bite, unable to control the raging hunger I felt since the moment I first saw the food. I hadn't realized just how starving I'd been, and the water he gave me to wash it all down made me feel more human. More capable of functioning.

I'd be able to run again. Logically, I knew asking Anderson for a ride would be my quickest way off the mountain, but I couldn't bring myself to ask for his help. Not with how pathetic I must have looked when he stumbled upon me in the woods.

The problem quickly became that he was attentive to me. He never turned his back, and waited on me hand and foot. How could I sneak out without a moment to myself?

I watched as he loaded the dishes into something he

called a dishwasher, shutting the lid and cranking the dial until the sound of rushing water filled the small kitchen.

"You don't have to wash them at all?" I asked, studying the device as he guided me up out of my chair at the kitchen table and to the back door.

"No. All I have to do is put them away," he laughed as I stepped out the door and into his backyard sanctuary. Some kind of wood flooring continued, giving a place to sit and enjoy the view of the sun rising in the morning. He had a fire pit too, but what caught my eye was the sight of his extensive gardens toward the forest edge.

"You garden?" I asked, excitement in my tone as I hurried down the steps and off the wooden structure.

"Not well, but I try," he said, following behind me. I spun back to smile at him, finding him staring at me with a little grin and his hands shoved into his pockets. The grass beneath my feet was thick and lush, undisturbed, unlike the heavily trodden ground I'd grown used to at the compound, where too many people walked on it daily for it to ever truly thrive.

Raised garden beds lined a walkway, and then beyond them a true vegetable garden was filled with the plants of summer.

I knelt on the ground next to the first raised bed, making sure my dress never touched the ground and eyed the small carrot greens that poked up from the dirt. I dug my hand into the dirt, letting it sift through my fingers as I studied it.

"Your soil is too sandy," I said. "See how light the color is? It should be rich. Deep brown. You didn't get this here."

"It came from the garden center in town," he said, leaning against a tree as he watched me. I brushed my hand on the grass to get the loose dirt off my skin before I stood.

"You bought dirt?" I asked, glancing around. "But you

have healthy dirt everywhere. This mountain is lush and full of life. You just have to nurture it a bit."

"Nurturing ain't my strongpoint, Baby," he responded, stepping closer to me. "Speaking of, we still need to get you fitted with that splint. Why don't we go back inside and do that?" I eyed the gardens ruefully. The plants in his vegetable garden were packed too tightly. The roots would never have the space they needed to grow. Everything in me wanted to repay his kindness by fixing them for him, but there was little I could do with the pulsing pain that radiated up my arm every time I moved it.

I should take the splint and leave. The gardens would never be mine.

Just like the man.

But as he came closer to me, I sucked in a ragged breath, then his chest touched mine. The thin material of my dress wasn't enough to block against the sensation of him touching me. Of him in my space and looking down at me with nothing but tenderness in his eyes. "You like to garden?" he asked, reaching up a hand and tucking a strand of hair behind my ear.

"It's the only thing I enjoy," I whispered.

"Well, Baby, we'll have to fix that. There's so much more to life than gardening, but it's yours, regardless." I was vaguely aware of his face coming closer to mine, of the way his lips hovered only a breath from mine and how his green eyes had speckles of brown throughout them when I got close enough.

"What's mine?" I whispered.

"Everything," he murmured, his lips brushing against mine for the first time. Hesitantly. he tested the contact, watching me to see if I would pull back. But I couldn't. I couldn't bear to take my lips away from his. Not with the way the slight pressure made me weak in my knees or with the way warmth radiated through my entire body from the slight contact. Seeming to understand what I didn't, he slid a hand into the curtain of my hair and cupped my head. Tilting it to the side and back, he closed his eyes and applied more pressure with his mouth.

The strangled groan that spilled free from my lips encouraged him until he teased the seam of my mouth with his tongue. With a gasp, I opened to him. The taste of him flooded my mouth, overrode my senses with something I didn't understand. He coaxed me into kissing him back until my good arm wrapped around the back of his neck and held on for what I could only describe as something miraculous.

When he finally pulled back, he touched his forehead to mine and smiled down at me. "Yeah, I thought as much," he said mysteriously.

"Huh?" I asked, my voice sounding just as dazed as I felt.

"Nothing, Baby," he chuckled. "You'll understand soon enough."

"Is that how it always is? Is it normal to feel hot? To be out of breath? The Disciples don't kiss. It's a sin to cross the line from duty into lust." I wanted to shut up. Wanted to stop talking about the *Children of Awe*, but what did I really have to talk about aside from them?

They'd made me who I was.

"No, Del. It isn't always the way it is between us. Only the lucky ones find this."

5

ANDERSON

She tasted like pure cane sugar. Sweet. Raw. Untouched. Untested.

She tasted like *mine.*

Staring down at her big grey eyes while she looked up at me, I knew there was nothing I wouldn't do to protect her. There was nothing that would stop me from making her mine and keeping her.

It didn't matter that, in some backwards religious cult, she had a husband she didn't want. It didn't matter who he might be or why she'd have married him in the first place.

All that mattered was the trust in her gaze as she studied me. The innocence that was mine to claim, and called to me as the other half of my soul.

The woman I thought didn't exist stood in my arms, and I'd burn the world to the ground before I ever let her go.

Deception wasn't one of the traits they seemed to teach in her community, because she was total shit when it came to hiding her intentions. I may not have known Del for long, but I recognized every impulse she got and the exact moment they told her to run.

I couldn't blame her, because I'd probably do the same thing if I thought I had a husband chasing me who would carve into my skin without hesitation. Not that she'd be his wife for long.

She'd be mine.

My phone rang in my pocket, interrupting our moment before I could try to make Del understand just how serious I was about what was happening between us. Pulling it out, I stared at the screen and loaded my security feeds from the woods. Something had tripped the motion sensor, and while it was probably just a stray deer who wandered too close, I needed to be sure. It wasn't often that deer got that close. The wire fence I put up deterred them.

The sight of a group of men trudging through my woods made my heart clench in my chest. Nobody lived up here except for the guys and I.

Nobody except the cult.

Del stared at the phone, her face going white with horror as she brought her good hand up to cover her mouth. She looked like she might be sick, but I forced through my concern. "In the house," I ordered, turning her to face the cabin. "I'm right behind you."

She hurried along the path, her pace increasing to an outright run in her urgency until she reached the door and flung it open quickly. I heaved out a sigh of relief once she was safely tucked inside, turning to scan the property once before I followed her.

My rifle hung by the door, and I grabbed it before settling in the living room. Del instantly came over and sat beside me. Her body trembled with her fear as I opened my laptop and loaded the security feeds to watch them skirt around the edges of the property. They hovered in the cover of the trees, looking for any signs of Del, undoubtedly.

There was nothing to find, not with my woman tucked safely next to me, but that didn't stop me from standing to pull the curtains closed just to be safe.

We watched, my heart in my throat, as one of the men pulled a scrap of white fabric off a tree branch. "Oh God," Del whispered, dropping her head to look at her feet. "Take me to town. That's the only way—"

"No. This is your home now and you're safe here." She stilled, not voicing her opinion on my words. I knew they'd come across overly harsh, but I wouldn't be able to be as gentle with her as I should until I knew exactly how far they would go in their hunt for her. Not until I knew she was safe.

Under any other circumstances, I'd have been quick to say that if a woman didn't want you and she ran away in the night, you let her go. But I couldn't say I wouldn't follow Del if she snuck out. The difference was, I would never hurt her the way he had.

She deserved the best. She'd get me instead.

We watched until the men faded back into the woods, the fabric of Del's dress clenched tightly in their hands. There was no doubt in my mind that they knew it was hers.

The only question was what they would do with that knowledge.

∞∞∞

Del poked at her pasta, barely touching it despite her initial excitement. It had quickly fizzled as night settled, and she couldn't contain her disappointment that she'd spent an entire day in a place where there was no doubt the *Children of Awe* would find her.

"Are they violent?" I asked, watching as those innocent

eyes rounded in surprise. "Aside from hurting women who can't defend themselves, anyway?"

"They have guns," she murmured, glancing at my rifle slung over the back of my chair. I'd noted her lack of concern over it and surmised as much. She was far too familiar with the sight of it to have never spent a deal of time around them.

"Are they decent shots?"

"I'm not sure. Women aren't allowed in the training grounds, but the hunters among them bring back meat every day. Jonathan says that keeping their skills sharp is an important part of protecting the community against invaders who don't understand. People who are too blinded by the lures of the Devil that they don't see the community serves God. I don't think Jonathan would risk himself, so I imagine they're decent with their guns to protect him."

"I'm no stranger to war, Del," I murmured, watching her eyes snap to mine. I hated the submission of her gaze on the floor, despised that it was so ingrained in her that she did it with me. I was not one of the bastards in the cult who taught her the most important thing she could be was obedient. I wanted her sweetness and her innocence, but I also wanted to watch her thrive in her newfound freedom.

I just wanted her to do it at my side.

"They have no idea what they got themselves into the moment I found you. Even if you weren't my woman, I'd protect you just because no woman should know the fear that sent you running in the night. I have the means and the skill, and you can settle here knowing they'll never touch you again." I thought she might question how I had the skill to protect her, and while I didn't want to explain the realities of war to my woman, I found I didn't have to in that moment.

"Your woman?" she asked instead, her grey eyes sparkling with what I hoped was desire. She wanted me. There was no doubt in my mind, but I didn't think Del understood it just yet.

"Yes, you're my woman."

"But I'm married," she argued, fiddling with the tape at the edges of the wrist brace we'd finally fitted her with. She had a persistent habit of wringing her hands, picking at the callouses as if she just wasn't used to sitting still. It was cute, except for the way her face twisted in pain each time.

"Do you want to be married to him?" She shook her head immediately. "Then we'll take care of it. You won't be married for long." I held out a hand, gently grasping hers when she put it in mine hesitantly. I guided her up the stairs to the loft, knowing that I would need her to have some privacy for what came next.

"Divorce is a sin," she sighed, her hand tightening in mine briefly, the only sign of her disappointment. I turned her so that her back was to the bed, bringing her hand up to my chest and squeezing gently until she looked at the connection.

"Nothing, and I mean absolutely nothing, between us could be a sin, Baby." She squeezed my hand back, slowly bringing that silver gaze back to mine with a small smile on her face. "Sometimes, people hide behind God to force their own beliefs on you. Sometimes they take advantage of faith to further their own purposes. I don't know what that cult taught you, but if there is a God, I can't believe he sent me to find you without reason. This right here is the reason, Del." I squeezed her hand for emphasis.

"You don't believe in God?" she whispered, and the confliction written on her face nearly cracked my heart in two. To be raised to believe in something absolutely and then betrayed so thoroughly had destroyed every sense of who she was and what she knew. All of it was written on her face, plain to see. She needed something to believe in.

"I believe in us. In here and now. In not wasting a minute of something that feels like the best thing that ever happened to me."

"I don't want to waste anything," she whispered. "I feel more alive with you than I ever have before. It scares me, but...I think I like it."

I moved our hands to her chest, drifting them down over her breasts and stomach as her breath caught, then rushed into her lungs. When I wrapped my fingers around the hem of her dress, she held it down tighter. "Do you trust me?" I whispered. I waited, giving her all the time she needed to make that decision for herself. I wouldn't be like him. Nothing would happen without her permission, but I was ready to taste my woman.

It seemed unfathomable that a few days ago I hadn't known she existed.

Slowly, she swallowed and nodded, releasing my hand. Guiding her dress up and over her head, I lifted it free from her body and tossed it onto the dresser. Del covered her breasts, and I allowed it as I sank to my knees in front of her and slid the panties down her legs. The bandage on her thigh nearly made my rage take control, but I quelled it for her sake.

Del didn't need my vengeance at that moment. She needed my love.

As soon as she was naked, I gave her my next instruction. "Go lay on the bed for me, Baby." She glanced over her shoulder at the soft surface, hesitating briefly before she drew in a deep breath and moved to do so. She climbed up on her knees, trying to hide her body as best she could, and then laid on her back with her legs clenched together tightly. I savored the moment, then said, "Touch yourself."

"I don't understand. Why would I touch myself?"

"Your body is yours, Del. Nobody can tell you what you can or cannot do with it. If you want to spread your legs and play with your pretty pussy, nobody has the right to tell you no. Take your body back."

She bit her lip, smiling sheepishly. "I don't know what a pussy is," she laughed. The sight of that smile, that sweet expression of her innocence, made my hard-on rage against the zipper of my jeans, but I denied it, to return the smile. Hers widened, faltering only when I stepped up next to the bed and took her hand in mine. Laying her fingers out against the skin of her stomach, I guided her hand down until it met the apex of her thighs. Nudging her legs apart, I encouraged her finger to brush against her little clit, grinning when her hips jolted under the touch. Encouraging two of her fingers to circle it, I loved every second of the way her hips writhed against the bed. There was no controlling that first touch, that first experience with everything that sex could be. When I drew my hand away, she worked herself with tiny, inexperienced fingers. Her chest flushed, pleasure coursing through her body. But never enough.

"Anderson," she moaned, and the sound of my name on her lips for the first time nearly snapped all my control.

"Do you want me to touch you?" I asked her.

"Please touch me," she whimpered, but she sat up straight when I moved around to the foot of the bed. Crawling between her spread legs, I moved her fingers away, eyeing her perfect pussy. Kissing the inside of her thigh, I worked my way toward it while she whimpered beneath me. The moment my lips touched her, she jolted and only my hands on top of her hips held her still. "Anderson," she protested, but it died off when I slid my tongue through her slit.

She gasped, her back arching on the bed as I worshiped her with my tongue. With my lips. With my teeth. She tasted like heaven, like the promise land had been delivered. Whether I deserved her or not, there was no letting her go once I'd had her taste on my tongue.

Sliding a finger through her, I placed it at her entrance and pushed inside slowly. Her walls clenched down, her gasp of surprise echoing through my head as I slowly pumped it in and out of her. Stretching her, I added a second finger, curling both to stroke her G-spot as I sucked her clit into my mouth and made her shatter beneath me with a cry. Crawling up next to her, I drew her into my arms and wrapped myself around her back.

It only took a few moments for her breathing to even out with sleep. I hated to leave her, but I knew there'd be no sleep for me for a few hours, not with the way a cold shower called my name.

6

DELIVERANCE

*H*alf numb to the world, I rolled over. My hand touched the cool sheets, instantly feeling the absence of Anderson's warmth. Peeling my eyes open, I clutched the sheet to my chest and glanced around the bedroom.

He was nowhere to be found, and something in me wilted. Waking up alone after my first experience of being touched was something I would have expected before, with Jonathon. With Anderson, I wanted more.

I stood from the bed and showered quickly, eventually dressing in my clothes from the day before and making my way downstairs in search of the man who'd left me sleeping.

A glance through the kitchen window confirmed he was outside fiddling with one of the solar lights he'd set up around the perimeter of the yard. I heaved a sigh of relief, content knowing that he was only working and hadn't changed his mind. It shouldn't have mattered.

It did.

Stepping back into the living room, I contemplated what to do with myself while I glanced around. His full bookcase under the stairs called to me, and I stepped over to it. My fingers ran along the spines, staring at the letters I didn't understand wistfully.

In another life, I would have liked to gather knowledge through the pages of a book. Maybe one day, I would.

My fingers caught on one spine in particular, the vivid green vines standing out against the white background so stunningly that I couldn't help but pull it from the shelf. I flipped it open, staring at the pictures of plants I both knew and didn't know, wishing I could read the names.

I jolted when the back door opened and Anderson stepped inside, turning to shove it back into its place on the shelf. He smiled at me, leaning against the wall after he turned the corner to the living room. "It's okay. You're welcome to read any of them. If you tell me what you like, we'll get you some more."

I slid the book onto the shelf but kept my fingers resting against the spine. Even though I couldn't seem to let it go, I could not look at him as I bit my lip shyly. "I don't know how," I admitted reluctantly.

"To read?" he asked, and I glanced over to him. He closed the distance between us, his fingers brushing against mine briefly before he pulled the book free and set it on the coffee table by the couch. "I'll teach you if you want. I promise."

"I sense a but coming," I said hesitantly, eyeing the book. It was something I wanted so desperately, but I had a feeling it came at a cost.

"No buts. Not really. Right now, we have to go to my buddy Cole's, but I'll teach you later," he laughed, tucking a strand of wet hair behind my ear. "You all set to go?"

I nodded, letting him guide me out of the house. The locks on the door were formidable and took a considerable amount of time to secure. All the while I watched him, only one thought plagued my mind.

I'd never been in a vehicle before.

The *Children of Awe* had a few, but the truck sitting in Anderson's driveway was much larger than anything they possessed. Women and children weren't allowed to leave the community, anyway. Given our conversation the day before where Anderson stressed that women could determine who touched them, I suspected that was why.

Jonathan couldn't have the young women of his community learning the truth. That outside that compound, an entire world existed where they could choose for themselves.

I wanted to have that right. I wanted it for me and for Noelle, and for any others who dreaded the day someone chose a husband for them.

When he finally finished, he brought me over to his truck and hefted me into the passenger seat, oblivious to the nerves I felt as soon as he closed me in. He climbed in next to me and some of that anxiety melted away. As much as I might not be able to stay with him, I had no doubts that Anderson wouldn't let anything hurt me. He reached over and pulled the strap over my shoulder and snapped it in next to me, doing the same for himself before he turned the key and the truck roared to life.

The vibrations jarred me as he eased down the driveway, but the moment he rested his hand on my thigh, it distracted me from my discomfort. The heat of it was like a brand as he maneuvered the truck through the winding mountain roads. We turned off the main road a few miles down, squashing my hesitant hope to slip away in town.

I cared for Anderson despite only knowing him briefly. Too much to let my problems come down on him. Besides, what kind of woman escaped a life where everything was decided for her and settled with the first man she saw? No matter the pulsing attraction I felt for him, no matter the way I wanted to curl up in his arms and let him protect me from all the things that scared me, I'd never seen anything beyond Mount Awe.

I hated that I had to find a man who made me weak right off. I despised that I couldn't stay.

"Where are we going?" I asked him, settling my hand down on top of his. The rough skin of his hard-labored hands echoed my own, feeling like a perfect match for me. The memory of how those hands had felt gripping my hips, with his arms wrapped around my thighs as he feasted on me, brought a flush to my cheeks.

He turned his palm over, grasping my hand in his. The massive size of him overwhelmed me, made me feel tiny compared to him. Even sitting in the seat next to me, he towered over me like a giant. "To my friend Coleman's. I didn't want to bring you into town until I trust you not to run, so he made a supply run to pick up some clothes and stuff for you. His shed is a little bigger, so we keep our extra gear at his place. I'll grab that while we're there."

"You think I'm going to run?" I whispered, studying him. His eyes left the road for a moment, a smirk transforming his face as he gave me the full force of that green stare.

"Baby, I know you're going to disappear the first chance you get. I just won't give you that opportunity." I stared at him long after he turned his attention back to the road, disbelief making me fumble over what to say.

"Don't you think it should be my choice? Isn't that what you said? Nobody gets to decide like that for me now?" His hand clenched around mine, his jaw tightening briefly. Still, he didn't take his eyes off the road.

I got the distinct impression I wouldn't like what I saw if
he did.

"Have I hurt you?"

"No. Of course not, but—"

"Did you not ask me to put my mouth on you last
night?" I blushed, not voicing my answer. We both knew I
had, as much as it embarrassed me to admit. "If you wanted
me to let you go, you should have never let me touch you,
Baby. Now I'm playing for keeps."

"I don't understand what that means," I sighed.

"It means I'm keeping you. I want it all, Del. Marriage.
Babies."

"What if I don't want that? That's the life they chose for
me in the *Children of Awe*. I want to see the world, Anderson. I want to get off this mountain." He pulled into the
dirt driveway, turning the truck off and unbuckling
himself.

Turning to face me suddenly, he unbuckled me and
captured my face between his massive hands. "Then we'll
wait for the babies, and I'll take you to see the world. I just
want to go with you, Del."

"This is your home. I can't ask you to leave it for me," I
whispered, feeling the starkness of his stare as he stripped
me open. "I don't know what kind of life I'm going to want. I
don't want to hurt you."

"You're my home now. If you don't want to hurt me, then
don't." His voice went deep, riddled with agony as he stroked
his thumb over my cheekbone. "I know you don't understand. It kills me you can't see how special this is between
us, because you have nothing to compare it to. Not every
relationship feels like this. Not every man will set you on fire
and feel like home all at the same time. Not every man will
look at you and think you were made for him, or that you're

the most beautiful woman he's ever seen. You're mine, Baby. And I'm yours."

I sniffled back my tears, choosing to echo his vulnerability with my own. "You're everything I could have dreamed of having, but I can't believe it. There's no way I stumbled through those woods and was picked up by a man who is going to love me the way I need."

"I fell in love with you the moment I saw you curled up on the ground in the woods, Del. I didn't even know your name, but I already knew you were mine in a way I never thought possible." Hope surged within me. Something I'd thought dead and gone, beaten out of me by the man my parents gave me to. There was nothing I wanted more than to feel it, but my mother's words echoed in my head.

Men who lived a life of sin would tell all lies to corrupt you.

While I didn't trust in my mother's words, there was something to be said of the improbability of falling in love in a day. In the community, love came after years of companionship.

It didn't sear you alive from the inside out with a single glance, and it definitely didn't make you abandon everything to follow someone you barely knew around the World.

I shook my head, although I wanted to believe those words more than anything. "You don't even know me. *I* don't even know me."

"I know you. Because I feel you in here." He took my hand, pressing it to his heart and holding it there for me to feel the steady rhythm. It thumped like the ticking of the clock in my room, strong and constant and reassuring all the same. I gaped at him until he leaned in and pressed his lips to mine gently, unsure what to say in the face of such a confession.

It was insane, but I wished that it could be true.

When he pulled back, he stepped out of the truck onto his ridiculously long legs, leaving me floundering as he came around to help me down. He didn't expect me to say it back. He said it himself. He knew that I didn't understand what we had.

The questions, the self-doubt, being so lost in life outside the *Children of Awe* was overwhelming. To have choices suddenly thrust upon me, how could I possibly know what was the *right* choice when I had no experience to base it on?

Anderson touched his lips to my forehead, smiling down at me with a breathtaking expression on his face. He stared at me like I was the only thing that mattered. Like all he saw was me when he had me in his arms.

Men couldn't lie about that, right?

Taking my hand, he led me to the breathtaking cabin at the top of the little hill that separated it from the driveway. I'd known Anderson said his friend's house was bigger, but I didn't appreciate just how *much* bigger it would be.

I preferred the coziness of Anderson's home—that he was almost always within sight.

I didn't know what that said about me leaving inevitably. If I didn't want to be out of sight in his house, being on the other side of the World seemed...

Devastating.

A man threw open the door and hurried down the steps, his blond hair gleaming in the sun and deep brown eyes shining as he approached us. Similar in size to Anderson, I had a moment to wonder if all men outside the compound were that large. "The Disciples were definitely not created equal," I whispered, making the man in front of me chuckle. Anderson's hand tightened on mine, not crossing over the threshold to be painful, but a warning no less.

"Del," he warned, his expression clearing when I turned wide eyes up to stare at him. "If you tell me you think he's handsome, I'll have no choice but to beat the shit out of him so he isn't so fucking cute anymore. I really don't want to have to do that."

I felt the warning in the words, but nothing could stop me from biting my lip and asking the most pressing question. "What's shit?"

The man waiting at the foot of the steps barked out a loud laugh, tossing his head back and clutching his chest as it shook. "Yeah, Anderson, what's shit?"

"What's fucking?" I asked, waiting for either of them to answer the question.

Anderson's cheeks pinked, and he shot a glance toward his friend cautiously before his gaze settled back on mine. "I'll show you later, okay?"

"You going to show her shit?" the other man asked, and I hated the feeling that I was on the outside of the joke. It was just another way that I didn't fit with Anderson.

"Okay," I whispered instead of voicing my hurt over being made fun of.

"This is Coleman. He's a buddy from work," Anderson said, introducing us. When we reached the bottom of the steps up to the porch, Coleman held out a hand to me. I stared at it, touching my hand to his with no clue what he wanted.

"It's a greeting," Coleman said, smirking at Anderson as he wrapped his hand around my waist and tugged me away from his friend.

"Let's just *not* put your grubby paws on my woman, yeah?"

"Dude, it's her hand," Coleman laughed, pulling his hand back and scrubbing it over his face to hide his smile.

"Do I look like I give a fuck? Don't touch her. Better yet, don't even look at her," Anderson said in his menacing voice.

With a kind smile for me in the face of Anderson's odd behavior, Coleman turned, striding for the house. Anderson pulled me to follow, and the inside of the cabin was even more breathtaking than the outside.

High ceilings. Wood beams. Beauty I'd never even dreamed of a few days before. "Coleman comes from a long line of rich men. He would have been disowned when he joined the Army, if his dad hadn't died before he could change the will. But Cole doesn't like anything that keeps him stuck sitting behind a desk. So the family investment firm just wasn't for him," Anderson explained, nodding his head to the only other man in the cabin. "That's Brick. He's from our Headquarters in the city."

"He's just up to make sure my systems are up to date," Coleman reassured me, watching the way Brick eyed me with distaste.

"It's true then, huh? You got yourself your very own virgin?" Brick asked, crossing his arms over his chest.

"Shut up, Brick," Anderson growled, moving to the corner to inspect the guns Coleman had lined up.

"The girls in the city will be so disappointed to know the mighty Anderson won't be coming to fuck them." I still didn't know what that word meant, but in that context, it seemed like it could only mean one thing.

Anderson growled out a curse, getting up in his friend's face with his fist at the collar of his shirt. I couldn't hear the words he spoke, but Brick's face twisted in disgust before he tugged out of Anderson's grip and stalked out of the cabin. Anderson sighed, turning to me and running his hand through his hair. "Baby—"

I shook my head, biting down on my tongue as I forced the lie from my mouth. "I'm fine." I waved him off. I hadn't thought he would be untouched. With what I knew of the world outside the *Children of Awe,* I knew that was nearly impossible. I'd never stopped to consider what that meant for me. Never thought about the fact that he could never be satisfied by a woman who had no clue how to please a man.

I hadn't even known it could feel good for a woman until he'd pushed me to touch myself.

"The clothes are on the couch, if you want to look at them." Coleman smiled, drawing me out of my contemplation. Anderson studied me as I moved to the stack, touching the floral prints with reverence. "Anderson said you like flowers."

"I love them. Flowers and color and anything not white," I admitted, watching as Anderson finally averted his attention back to studying the weapons and whatever other supplies he needed to secure his property against the people who wanted to drag me back.

Without the burden of his stare on me, I felt like my lungs could finally get a full breath.

I needed to get away from him before I lost all my common sense, because even while he tried to focus on everything Coleman showed him, his attention kept coming back to me.

He glared whenever Coleman glanced my way until I finally sighed and moved over to them. Inserting myself into Anderson's side, I snuggled in and wondered how I'd ended up with the one man who couldn't stop looking at me long enough for me to run.

*D*el's foot tapped impatiently, and she delicately picked at the skin of her fingertips. Her body hummed with the steady energy of a woman who needed to move. With her ass perched on the edge of the sectional sofa, she looked every bit the type who didn't know the first thing about getting comfortable. I shook my head with a brief grin, turning back to the pot I needed to scrub.

"I can do that," she said, jumping to her feet.

Spinning, I pointed a scolding finger in her direction. "What you need to do is rest. Drink the rest of that water, get comfortable, and take a nap."

"A nap?" she whispered, raising her eyebrows at me. "Babies nap. I may not understand why you call me Baby, but even I know that I'm not *actually* one."

I dropped my head forward, chuckling into my shirt. It seemed so strange to have my woman understand me, but still not really understand me at the same time. "You are definitely not a baby," I sighed, drying my hands on a dish towel and moving to sit beside her on the couch. I drew her into my arms, settling back against the cushion and dragging her with me. Careful not to jostle her wrist, I held her tight enough that she had no choice but to rest her head on my chest. With her head right above my heart, she was right where she belonged. My world felt complete with her in it.

"Then why call me that?" There was no judgement to her tone, only curiosity and a vague sense of annoyance. I couldn't imagine how difficult it must have been to be thrown into the world of American Slang.

"It's a term of endearment. Some people call their spouse Baby," I explained, tucking a strand of dark hair behind her ear as she turned her face up to look at me. That small mouth pressed tightly together as she mulled over my words.

"So I should call you Baby?"

"You could if you wanted to," I said, trying to keep my voice neutral.

Eventually she wrinkled her nose and shook her head, bringing me a sigh of relief. "I don't know what to call you, but Baby isn't it."

"You could call me your man," I said, pausing before deciding to push her just a bit. Being patient with Deliverance didn't come easy, not when I knew what I wanted without a doubt. I couldn't wait forever for her to catch up to me. "Or if my buddy pulls through with the Annulment, you could call me Husband."

She stilled in my arms, averting her gaze. My arms tightened around her, holding her still as she debated with herself internally. Her body felt like a war zone in my hold, the struggle between her warring desires something that I could feel through her. "I'm not ready for that," she whispered finally, and I took it as the win it was. She didn't say that she couldn't. She didn't say that she'd leave me.

"I need you to get there, Baby," I said. "Can you do that for me?"

There was a stretch of silence between us as I waited for her answer. Finally, she nodded. "Okay," she murmured, and I didn't bother trying to control the broad grin that crossed my face before I tugged her up closer and kissed her.

The first touch of my lips on hers always knocked me breathless. Like a sucker punch to the gut every single time. Her air and my air mixed, blending into something new that felt unique as we each left *I* behind and became *us*. I snagged her hips, dragging her on top of me until her knees spread around my hips and her sweetness touched the ridge of my cock through my jeans. She gasped into my mouth, her hips rocking involuntarily at the first spark of friction.

I wasn't even sure she was aware she did it as I held her head steady with a hand buried in the curtain of her straight hair. She could explore my body however she felt comfortable, because there was no way I'd be able to hold out much longer.

I needed to be inside my woman.

I just had to hope she would want that as much as I did.

She moaned into my mouth when I reached between her legs, stroking her over the fabric of her panties. Pulling back sharply, she buried her face in my neck. "Oh," she sighed.

Encouraging her to sit up, I brought her hands to my shirt. Placing those dainty, calloused fingers at the top button, I watched indecision war in her eyes before she ground her little pussy down harder on my fingers and slowly unhooked that first button.

The second followed without prompting. Her eyes narrowed on the small expanse of skin she revealed in the center of my chest. Her fingers brushed against it as she moved down farther, following the trail of buttons on the flannel I'd thrown on, when I'd thought I could bring myself to separate from Del long enough to go outside and set up additional security. The light, innocent touch went straight to my cock, making it twitch in my jeans more enthusiastically than any of the women in my past had managed.

None of them had been Del, and my dick knew it as well as I did.

With the shirt unbuttoned all the way, she pushed the fabric away from my chest. Staring down at my torso, she ran tentative fingers in a path from the light hair at my collarbone down to the happy trail below my belly button.

Gliding back up, she traced a circle around one of the scars on my stomach. Then the next, and then to the bullet-shaped scar on my shoulder. She bit her bottom lip briefly, then leaned forward and touched her mouth to the marks one by one. My abs rippled as her mouth hovered over the one on my lower abdomen. Just her breath was the sweetest torment.

She jolted off my lap at the sound of my perimeter alarm resounding through the cabin. "Fuck," I cursed, flipping my laptop open and bringing up the feeds for my cameras. At the edge of the driveway, a group of men wearing all white hopped out of the front of the truck. Del stared at the screen, wringing her hands despite the pain it must have caused her wrist.

It wasn't until the passenger door swung open and a middle-aged man climbed out that her body went still with terror. With dark hair and a freshly shaven face, he might have radiated charm if it wasn't for the scowl on his face as he looked up the driveway. "Who is he?" I asked Del, not taking my eyes off the man as he started up the dirt path.

"Jonathan," she mumbled, rising to her feet. She glanced

around the space, eying the back door like she might bolt. "I can't go back," she whispered, clenching her eyes shut as if the thought was physically painful. I didn't have a hard time believing it was, knowing what he'd do to her as punishment for running.

"Hey," I said, standing and grasping her face in my hands. "I won't let anybody hurt you. Just trust me."

Panic filled her eyes, but she nodded against the urge to flee. "Okay," she said hastily.

"Jonathan is the leader of the *Children of Awe*, yeah? Why would he come himself? Did you take anything with you that they'd want back?" I asked, needing all the information at my disposal before I dealt with him. I couldn't negotiate with a man when I didn't know the variables. She bit her lip, her face twisting, but she remained silent. "Del," I warned.

"Jonathan came because he's my husband," she whispered, her voice laced with shame. "I'm his First Wife. The one he believes God blessed him with to provide him sons. He'll see my leaving as an affront to God, Anderson."

I stared at her for a moment as the pieces snapped into place. The signs had all been there. The subtle hints, but she'd never outright said that the Jonathan she spoke of as a messenger of God was the man who hurt her. "*Jesus.* Fuck." The bastard had to be three times her age from what I'd seen in my research while she slept.

"Please, don't let him—"

"Shh. Nobody's going to take you away from me. Go upstairs to the loft. Stay out of sight. For now, we assume they don't know you're here. Go." I told her, kissing her briefly and watching as she turned and fled up the stairs.

Watching the driveway feed, I tore the shirt off my shoulders. I wouldn't have time to button it, and nothing looked more like I had a woman in my house than answering the door in an unbuttoned shirt. The knock on the door seemed to vibrate through the small cabin, and I waited a few moments before I made my way to it.

With a final glance up to the loft to make sure Del was out of sight, I drew in a deep breath to prepare myself for a conversation with the man who'd hurt her.

I wanted to strangle him. To watch the life bleed from his eyes and hear him scream the way I imagined Del had when he'd carved into her with his knife. Instead, I plastered a fake smile on my face and pulled the door open.

His scowl was gone, replaced by a smile filled with perfect teeth and a face that appeared younger than I knew he must be. Deep eyes stared back at me, sparkling as he tried to hide his glance around the inside of the cabin. "Can I help you?" I asked.

I resisted the urge to shudder when his eyes met mine fully, something so twisted and demented lurking in the depths of them that I knew instantly Del had every right to be afraid for her life. He would hurt her again. He would break her and mold her into an entirely new and obedient woman of his making. The thought of Del so shattered, only pieces of herself remaining hidden below the surface, made my fists clench at my side.

"I hope so," he said, that grin going even wider as he studied me. "I seem to have lost my wife. We went for a romantic stroll in the woods a few days ago for some privacy, and we were separated. I haven't seen her since, and I'm truly worried for her. The woods are a dangerous place, and I hate to think what might have happened to her."

"I haven't seen her," I grunted, barely controlling my rage. The lying sack of shit probably could have sold the lie to most people, making them think his poor wife was lost in the woods and he was only a concerned husband instead of the abusive piece of shit he really was.

"How do you know? I haven't told you what she looks like."

"Do I look like I get many visitors?" I forced a chuckle. "Not up here. Especially not women. I haven't seen a single woman since I went into town at the base weeks ago."

"We found this in the woods just outside your fence," he said with a patient sigh, holding up the scrap of white material we'd watched the others pull from the tree branch.

"Maybe she passed by, but I haven't seen her. Have you checked the town? That's where I'd go if I got lost," I suggested.

"I have people scouring the town already, yes. No sign of her, I'm afraid." He sighed again, tucking the fabric into the pocket of his linen pants.

"I hope she turns up safe," I said, curling my fingers around the door to signal our conversation had ended.

He nodded, but I didn't think for a moment he believed my bullshit. "If you see her, tell her she'd best come home. I'll be waiting."

"I'll be sure to let her know. If I see her." I smiled tightly, closing the door. Del poked her head out, but I held up a finger to tell her to stay put. I wanted some distance between that fuck and my woman first.

8

DELIVERANCE

*W*aiting for Anderson after his conversation with Jonathan felt like being torn into a hundred pieces and waiting to see if he'd bother to put me back together.

I'd never meant to keep that my marriage was to Jonathan a secret. I didn't even think I had, really, but the shock on his Anderson's face when I admitted the truth was painfully obvious.

Lies were a sin. Secrets were a sin.

All the sins I'd committed since leaving the community repeated in my head. The indoctrination of my upbringing stayed with me in a way I knew it would be years before I managed to rid myself of the haunting voice of my mother or the echo of Jonathan's prayers in the Church every morning.

I just wanted it to stop.

I stood from the floor when Anderson finally appeared at the top of the stairs, his steps closing the gap between us quickly. "You somehow forgot to mention that your husband is the leader of the *Children of Awe*."

"I told you he would never let me go," I whispered back. "I didn't think his name mattered."

"There's a big difference between one man being scorned and an entire community of lunatics thinking you're destined to bring forth the next messenger of God, Del," he snapped. I flinched back from the brutal bite to his words. Anderson had never been harsh with me, never shown me even a moment of anger.

He ran a hand through his hair, sighing out his frustration. "Come here," he ordered.

I hurried forward immediately, wrapping my arms around his waist and pressing tightly into his chest for comfort. I'd never known how perfect it could feel to be wrapped in a pair of strong arms.

To simply be held because someone loved me.

I'd never known what it was to be loved at all.

"I know this situation is difficult for you, but you've got to be honest with me for us to work. I don't know your past, and you don't know mine. All we know is what we tell one another. I think in your little community, you got so used to people just knowing every detail of your life that you forgot how to talk about it," he said against the top of my head.

"I don't want to talk about it. My life there." I paused, mulling over the words. "There were too many rules. Idleness is a sin, because it means you are wasting time you could spend serving God and the community. The need to be moving and working constantly kept us largely isolated, despite being together all the time."

"How did you end up married to Jonathan?" he asked, his fists tightening against my spine.

"My mother told me he would take a new wife, and that there were rumors it would be me. My father is good friends with Jonathan, so I suspect they discussed the possibility of me. That same day Jonathan announced we would marry the next night." Anderson guided me over to the bed, sitting down on the edge next to me. My fingers trailed circles over the bare skin of his arm, remembering the way his torso and the ridges there had felt under my hands. I wanted to explore him more.

I wanted to be with Anderson. The confliction in me was that part of the reason I wanted to be with him was only so I could choose. I could make a choice and give my body to someone who wasn't Jonathan.

If sex with Anderson was a sin, then I never wanted to be righteous.

"That simple? He decides he wants you and you don't get a say?" Anderson growled.

"Typically, my father would have to agree to the marriage," I admitted. "But given who Jonathan is, nobody would ever think to deny him."

"Even though he's your father's age."

"Yes. To serve him is to serve God—"

"Do *not* talk to me about serving him. You will never touch him," Anderson warned.

"I don't want to touch him," I assured him, even though it was made obvious by the fact that I ran. "You're the only one I want." I blushed, taking his hand off my bare thigh and moving it up my dress. Something about the fact that Anderson had talked to Jonathan with my touch on his skin, with my taste in his mouth and my sex on his fingers, fulfilled a dark urge I didn't understand.

I wanted Anderson to take me. To claim me and make me his.

"Baby," he warned. "We have to talk about this."

"I don't want to talk at all." I smiled, heat warming my cheeks as he studied me. "I want to be yours." Even if it may not last. I still had a future, an uncertain one at that, that called to me despite my growing affection for Anderson.

"You already are," he murmured, returning my smile with a confident one of his own. Grasping the hem of my dress, he tugged it up and over my head. He stood us up only long enough to strip off my underwear, and then he laid me down in the center of the bed gently. My fingers went to the button of his jeans, freeing it and sliding down the zipper slowly.

He grinned at the tremble in them, the nerves I couldn't control. Then he shoved the jeans down his thighs, corded with muscle, kicking them off his ankles less than gracefully.

His length hung heavy between us, seeming larger than I'd considered possible in all my considerations of what a man might look like when he took off his clothes. I knew the logistics of sex, but only just. Only enough to serve my husband one day.

He was too big to fit.

He smirked down at me, dropping his mouth to the space between my breasts and holding my eyes as he kissed me. I writhed beneath him, moaning his name when he drew one pebbled nipple into his mouth and sucked.

Fingers played between my legs, building me closer and closer to an explosion of the senses that I both wanted and dreaded. He pumped a finger inside me. Then a second. Stretching me while his thumb rubbed at the apex of me.

When he drew his hand away, I sucked in a ragged gasp. I'd been so close, but the smile in his eyes was knowing. "You come when I'm inside you this time," he murmured, pressing his lips to mine briefly.

The pressure of him touched my core, sliding through the outside of me where I was swollen and needy for him.

With a final study of my face, he reached between us, rubbing the tip of himself along me briefly.

Then he guided himself inside me. My breath hitched, feeling every inch of him as he rocked his hips and pushed through tender and tight tissue slowly. Wrapping a hand around the back of my neck, he tilted my head up to look in my eyes and shoved through the barrier inside me.

Burning quickly pinched at my insides, but he soothed it with the sweet murmur of his voice and the green of his eyes on mine. Rocking in and out in short pulses of his hips, he took what I gave inch by inch until nothing existed but him. But the place where we connected and the feeling of fullness that settled over me. "Anderson," I whispered.

"I know, Baby. I feel it too." He took my hands in his, lacing his fingers with mine and pinning them to the bed as he thrust in and out in a steadier rhythm. He kissed me, emotion tangling me into a mess of contradictions. My body heated, and the feel of him inside me so completely sent me spiraling towards the edge like he'd done the day before. "That feeling is love, Del. Because you love me too. You just have to admit it to yourself," he whispered, with his lips at my ear. He released my hands, sliding one down my body until he grasped the back of my thigh and shoved my leg high and wide.

His thrusts turned to pounding, taking me with deep rolls of his hips that made me cry out. My breasts shook with the force of each one, and I rolled my head to the side. "Nobody else will ever give you this," he growled. "Nobody but me will make you feel this way."

"Anderson," I whimpered, reaching out for him. The fear of me leaving him showed in every etched line on his perfect face. He took my hand, using it to flip me over to my stomach.

His hands at my hips drew me up to my hands and knees, and then he surged back inside with a sharp snap of his hips. "Oh, God!" One hand buried in my hair, tangling it around his fist and drawing me up until my back pressed against his chest. Until his face buried in my neck and he nipped the delicate skin there.

He let my hair loose finally, wrapping that hand around the front of my throat and pressing down. He gave me no reprieve from the frantic energy of his thrusts. From the pounding of him inside me. The other hand moved between my thighs, touching the place where he battered into me and wrapping his fingers around himself. "So fucking tight, Baby. So fucking *mine.*"

"Please," I begged as the heel of his palm ground against that spot at the top of me that drove me mad.

"Tell me you love me," he growled into my neck, biting the spot between my neck and my shoulder roughly. "Tell me or I'll fuck you until you do."

So this was what fuck meant.

"I can't," I pleaded.

"You will." Fingers moved through me, spreading me open as he made his way to that bundle of nerves and rubbed them more directly. "Because I love you, Baby. I won't accept anything less from you."

He kept at it, fucking and circling the bundle like he had all day, but the grunts of his exertion grew with each passing moment. It thrilled me to know that even as he tormented me, it was torture for him too.

That he took solace in my body as much as I found myself in his. I wasn't a Child of Mount Awe when he put his hands on me. I was a woman set aflame by a man who loved her irrationally. Inexplicably.

"I love you," I whimpered finally, conceding to his insane

demands. Part of me wished I could taste a lie on my tongue, that I'd know they weren't true. But I suspected they were the truest words I'd ever spoken.

And all the more terrifying for it.

The hand at my throat turned my head, then he was devouring my lips in a kiss that stripped away all semblance of who I'd been before.

He erased Deliverance with his kiss and claimed Del as his.

His woman. His life.

His everything.

He swallowed my cry as I spasmed around him, light flooding my senses. His own roar erupted behind me, echoing through the cabin and making the walls vibrate as heat flooded me.

My breath came in ragged gasps as vision returned. Anderson eased me down onto the bed, curling up behind me and never breaking our connection.

He stayed locked inside me longer than it took for me to fall asleep.

*T*he axe came down on the log, splitting it in half with ease. Sweat trickled down my spine, the afternoon sun beating down on me. I hoped Del wasn't a light sleeper under normal circumstances, given my inability to sleep past five in the morning. Too many years in the military meant early wake up was as much a part of me as the scars on my body.

As well as the ones on my soul from all the friends lost.

Another *thunk* of wood splitting, another vent of my rage at the prospect of losing Del. She was everything I could have ever dreamed of having for myself and then some.

She loved me. Sexually manipulated into the confession or not, I felt the weight of it in my soul. The truth of it.

If only I could make her sit still long enough for her wrist to heal and for her body to recover from everything she'd put it through in her escape. Not to mention the beating she'd taken before she fled. As if summoned, she poked her head out the back door cautiously. Drowning in my flannel shirt, she looked even smaller for the way it went to the middle of her thighs. She crossed her arms over her chest, looking uncomfortable. As if she'd done something wrong by wearing my shirt, when the reality was I'd set that shirt aside and never wash it if I didn't have the real, live woman waiting for me.

We had a lifetime of her waking up and putting on my shirts ahead of us.

"Are you hungry? I can cook breakfast," she said, her voice barely carrying to me even though my chopping block wasn't far from the house.

Swinging the axe down, I let the block hold it and made my way to her. Stroking a thumb over her cheekbone, I tilted her face up to mine and caressed her mouth with mine softly. "I'll be in to cook in a minute. Now get your sexy ass back in the house," I warned her, turning her on her heel and giving said ass a little swat in warning. She jolted, rounding to gape at me.

We'd have to work her into the kink of spankings, it seemed. I didn't imagine they were a sexual thing in the cult. Though one never knew, considering the demented fuck who ran it.

"I can't stay cooped up inside forever, you know," she whispered, eying the woods behind the house. "I'll go stir crazy."

"Let's just be cautious until the marriage is annulled. I'll feel better when he doesn't have a leg to stand on or any claim over you." She nodded, pursing her lips like she didn't like it but couldn't argue with that.

Turning on her heel, she walked toward house and I watched her ass until the door closed behind her and cut off my view. My eyes went to the woods, hating that I had to keep my woman inside when she loved being outdoors as much as I did.

Soon, she'd be free.

Soon, she'd be mine entirely.

∞∞∞

Del ate like she was starved. Under any other circumstances, it might have worried me that she was so hungry. I might have been pissed at myself for not feeding her enough.

Instead, the knowledge that the voracious hunger came from our lovemaking the night before only filled me with pride.

She devoured her eggs and worshipped her bacon like she'd never seen it before. It occurred to me that she probably hadn't. That was, if nothing else, just another sad indicator of the sheltered life she'd had. To never have bacon should have been a crime in itself.

Teaching a young girl that it was acceptable for her father to decide who she married, without even an inkling of permission from her, was another.

Carving into a woman's flesh when she disobeyed would buy you a death sentence, in my book.

As soon as she'd finished, I set the plates on the coffee table and grabbed the book on plants. It wasn't the best book to teach her to read on, admittedly, but it would do for starting to see if she knew her alphabet. "We'll get you something simpler when we go to town eventually, but to start, do you know your letters?"

"No," she whispered, and my fury over how they'd kept her so isolated only grew. She couldn't even spell her name, because of their desire to keep her ignorant and desperate.

I pointed to a letter on the first page. "This is an A." She stared at it with intrigued grey eyes, studying the lines intently.

"A tent with a line," she said with a nod. "A."

"Apple starts with A. So what sound does it make?"

She rolled her lips around as she considered, a blush spreading over her chest and up her cheeks. "Apple," she said slowly. "Ap?"

"Ah," I corrected with a smile. "But that was close."

The shrill sound of the alarm rang through the house, and I cursed and jumped to my laptop, set up on the coffee table in the living room. On my screen, Jonathan strolled up the driveway, not a care in the world as he slid his hands into the pockets of his linen pants and pulled out a piece of paper. When he reached the steps up to the porch, he turned and looked directly at the camera with a sinister, knowing smile that made my blood run cold.

He knew.

Without a doubt, he knew Del was in the house with me.

The paper he slid under the door stared back at me like something from a horror movie, but Del never took her eyes off the laptop screen as Jonathan blew a kiss at the camera. Her face went white, her skin losing all traces of the radiant glow I'd seen on her for just a few passing moments that morning. Once he retreated down the steps and climbed into the truck at the foot of the driveway, I went to the door and picked up the note.

"*All sinners must repent. Return my wife by sunset, or I'll take her myself,*" I read aloud, turning to look back at Del. She was already on her feet, surging for the back door in her haste to get out. "Del!" I shouted, leaping over the coffee table and following her as quickly as I could.

Her shrill scream filled the cabin in response as she willed her legs to make it to the door before I caught her. But my legs were much longer than hers, my willpower much stronger.

Nothing would take her from me. Not even her own fear.

"No!" she yelled when my arms wrapped around her waist. Tiny fists struck my arms, shoving and digging her short nails in to get me to release her.

"Calm down," I snarled in her ear, catching her arms in my grip and pinning them to her body as I shuffled her to the couch. She kicked and screamed like a banshee, my sweet and soft Del replaced by a wild hellion determined to get free.

Tossing her to the couch and maneuvering her onto her back, I covered her with my body until she had no chance of escaping me. "I can't stay!" she begged, shaking her head from side to side with wide eyes. "There are too many of them. I won't let you put yourself in danger for me."

"Woman, I'm a big boy. Stop hiding behind the excuse of wanting to protect me. I've fought worse than Jonathan and his *Children of Awe*. I'll call my guys in, and we will knock them on their asses."

"But—"

"If I'd let you go into the city, they'd already have you. You need to realize you're much safer with me than you are on your own. Stop fighting it," I warned her.

She paused, looking up at me with wide grey eyes and hesitation written all over the tense lines of her face. "If I don't leave now, I never will."

My body went solid, fury thrumming through my body in a solid twist of pain. "That ship sailed when you took me inside you. When you told me you loved me. When you let me come inside you. Fuck's sake woman, you could already be pregnant; are you shitting me right now?"

The confusion in her eyes did nothing to appease the rage I felt that she would still consider leaving me. She knew she had to do it soon because of what was growing between us. Nothing was more frustrating than, knowing her feelings for me scared the hell out of her, not being able to do a damn thing to reassure her it would all be okay. "I will not lose you," I barked at her.

"Anderson," she whispered, staring up at me with tears in her eyes. The sadness there felt like a punch to the gut, but I was in no place to be gentle with her in that moment.

"I'm going to put up the traps I got from Coleman and call the guys. Lock the door behind me and stay fucking put, Del. I mean it. You leave this house, and I will hunt you down."

I jumped up from the couch, swinging the pack of traps and cameras over my shoulder as I grabbed my rifle.

"Anderson," Del whispered at the last second, sitting up and staring at me in the open doorway. "I do love you. I just- I can't go back."

"You won't, Baby. Over my dead body. I'll be back soon. Do not open this door for anyone but me or Cole, got it?" She nodded, and I turned and stalked out the back door. I had booby traps to set for some shit stains who needed to be shown just what happened when someone fucked with what was *mine*.

*I*n his absence, I paced around the cabin, feeling nothing but shame for the way I'd treated Anderson. If I stopped to think about what might be out there waiting for me in the rest of the World, I couldn't think of one thing that I wanted more than the way I felt with him.

He made me real.

He made me *feel*.

Maybe the best solution would be both of us leaving the mountain for a while and waiting for Jonathan to give up. But I just couldn't bring myself to take Anderson away from his home. He loved nature and the sanctuary of his cabin. The closeness of his friend Coleman and the others they'd mentioned in passing while he gathered supplies.

Moving into the kitchen, I tugged the refrigerator open and used my left hand to grab the jug of water Anderson kept there. The weight of it felt enormous to my weaker side, but the fracture in my right rendered me useless. I nearly dumped over my glass when I tried to pour it.

The sudden shrill of Anderson's perimeter alarms sounding through the house was the final straw to my lack of coordination. Water sloshed all over the counter and floor, tipping the glass until it fell and shattered against the tile at my feet.

I slipped in the water in my haste to get to Anderson's laptop on the coffee table, but it was closed. I suddenly wished I'd pushed for him to teach me how to use the thing. His phone was nowhere in sight, and I hoped to God that meant he would hear the alarm. That he'd know either he'd tripped it and scared me, or that someone else was on the property.

I'd wanted to know who I was on my own?

I was *nothing* without Anderson. I needed him like the very next breath in my lungs. I needed the safety and comfort of his arms wrapped around me and his calm, stern voice telling me what to do.

Minutes passed with me staring at the closed laptop and wondering what to do. My indecision plagued me; my inability to make choices for myself poking at me like a taunt.

How had I ever thought I could exist out in the real world?

I couldn't even make a single decision without Anderson's help.

Footsteps echoed on the porch, and I listened for a moment. More footsteps. More than one person.

I bolted to the back of the cabin, throwing open the closet door and pulling it closed behind me. Hiding behind Anderson's bulky winter jackets, I made myself as small as possible and hid in the mound of winter clothes and boots on the floor. Men were unorganized, and frankly disgusting, but I'd never thought I could be pleased with that like I was the moment the weight settled on top of me and hid my legs.

I could barely hear the voices outside from my place in the closet. Only the soft murmur of what I suspected had to be men shouting orders at one another. They continued, until one of the voices rose in pitch finally, his frustration broadcasting even through the barriers between us.

Glass shattered in the living room, the distinct sound of it echoing through the cabin. I covered my mouth with my hand, muting the shrill scream of pure terror before it could escape.

More glass clinking, and then there were footsteps inside the house itself.

Tears burned my eyes, the question echoing in my head.

Is Anderson hurt?

I trembled in my hiding spot, the sound of men invading his home stroking the flame of anger inside me. With each thump of furniture and God knows what being thrown around, it burned higher and higher within me.

Until I wanted nothing more than to look Jonathan in the eye and make him bleed the way he'd bled me. The way he'd hurt Anderson by breaking his sanctuary from the world. Still, I knew from the depths of my soul that all the stuff in that sanctuary would be replaceable to Anderson.

I would not.

That knowledge was the only thing that kept me tucked safely in the closet while they ravaged the cabin I'd begun to think of as my new home. "Come out, my wife. Let me rescue you from sin," Jonathan called out. His arrogance and lack of concern that Anderson might come only increased my concern for him.

When there was still no sign of Anderson, my terror for him became unbearable. If something happened to him because of me, I would never forgive myself. I'd deserve everything Jonathan did to me as penance for the sin of endangering the only man worth my love.

The closet door opened suddenly, and I froze in my hiding space, hoping they would find no one and walk away. Those hopes were dashed when an arm roughly swept the coats to the side, revealing my hiding place so instantly I gasped when the cruel brown eyes of a boy I'd grown up with stared back at me.

"Peter!" I pleaded, flinching when he dove forward and a harsh hand grabbed me by the hair. "Let go of me!" I screamed, tugging at the fingers yanking my scalp. Pain exploded through my head. Pulling. Tearing my hair by the roots and using it as motivation to make me rise to my feet and follow.

The pressure was enough to send me lurching to my feet. Once he positioned himself behind me, the pain eased slightly. The damage was done however, as he lifted me off my feet with an arm around my waist and shuffled me into the living room. Kicking my legs and panting through the effort, I screamed as loud as I could.

Hoping that the broken window next to the couch would carry the sound to wherever Anderson was. Praying he would hear me.

Jonathan rounded the back of the couch slowly, stepping into the space in front of me while I kicked my legs at him futilely. He swatted them down to the floor, positioning himself in front of me while Peter held me still with a tighter grip on my hair that made my eyes water.

"Hello, wife," Jonathan murmured, reaching up a hand to touch my cheek delicately. As if I was precious to him. As if I was more than just a commodity and something to breed. His hand trailed down over Anderson's shirt, through the valley between my breasts, until his soft fingers toyed with the hem at my thigh while I struggled against the skin to skin contact. "Such a shame," he whispered, bringing striking hazel eyes up to study my face. "You always were my favorite. Even as a little girl, you promised so much potential." My skin crawled. Goosebumps slithering over my skin at the sick confession. Saliva pooled in my mouth, accompanying the urge to vomit in his face. "Did you give him what belongs to me?" he asked, his voice deepening to his attempt at a growl. In contrast with the fierce masculinity I'd come to expect from Anderson, for the first time I saw how weak Jonathan was.

How pathetic.

I kicked a leg into the side of his calf, taking whatever I could. His glare turned harsh for a moment, before he turned his eyes away from mine to address the other men in the room as much as he spoke to me. "He's corrupted you. My poor, obedient wife led to temptation by the Devil himself."

I smirked back at him, only barely resisting the urge to peel my lips back from my teeth and snarl at him like a wild animal. It was how I felt in those moments. Trapped. Caged.

And I realized that Anderson had shown me true freedom, even while keeping me with him. He'd given me the freedom to be me.

"Was I so obedient when I refused to *fuck* you on our wedding night?" I announced, speaking the words loud enough to make sure all his men heard his failure. His inability to seduce his young wife should have brought him shame, but the men of the *Children of Awe* didn't seduce. They took, feeling it was their right. He only grinned back at me, calculation moving through his eyes as he studied my struggling form. I continued, "The only one who is corrupted is you. Corrupted by your own greed and the lies you tell each and every one of your Disciples."

The accusation made the first trace of unease trickle over his face, his jaw slacking just enough to show the comment bothered him. He leaned in, touching his lips to the shell of my ear. "I'll very much enjoy rebreaking you."

"You never broke me in the first place," I growled back. "I'll escape every chance I get. Do you think your reputation can survive a wife who doesn't want you? That your followers will continually support your chasing down a woman who wants nothing to do with your version of God, while you shun the others who would?"

He pulled his face back from my ear finally, a slow grin transforming his deceptively handsome face. "Noelle misses you," he said, the strike hitting me directly in the center of my chest. I didn't know her well, but I knew enough about her life now to feel responsible for her suffering. I was free. She was not. "She's been finding it...difficult to cope with my worry for you. If you care for her at all, you'll come home so my righteous fury can go to the person who deserves it." I stilled, hearing the threat in those words for what it was. The others might have remained oblivious, but I knew without a doubt that he took his anger with me out on her every night in the privacy of his home.

Because she'd helped me escape.

I couldn't just leave her to continue to suffer the punishments meant for me. I opened my mouth, ready to condemn him for the monster he was.

A muffled *thunk* echoed through the mostly quiet room, and the pressure on my scalp suddenly released as fluid splashed onto the back of my neck. The weight of Peter collapsing nearly dragged me to the floor, and only Jonathan reaching out and pulling me into his embrace stopped my fall. Placing his back to the wall, he positioned me in front of him, facing out.

My eyes landed on Peter's body on the floor. It wasn't the first time I'd seen one.

But it *was* the first time I saw the inside of a head.

*M*ost of them scattered with Cole's first shot. Their blind loyalty to their leader only lasted so long in the face of a bullet to the brain.

Nobody came into my home and put their hands on my woman.

I only regretted that I hadn't been the one to fire the shot. Instead, I cut my way through the Disciples who didn't flee, getting closer and closer to Del with every shot from my pistol and every swing of the blade in my hand.

I'd known the moment they touched my property, gotten the alarm the moment they dared to step into my territory.

But there'd been two dozen of them, and only one of me. Even as skilled as I was, those numbers were not in my favor. I was no good to Del dead.

So, I'd had to make the painful decision to call Coleman and to take a stealthy approach, picking at the edges of their numbers slowly and carefully. With the cameras and security system, I'd know the moment they tried to take her from the house.

Her scream echoing through the newly fallen night

would haunt my dreams for the rest of my life. Just like the scream that came after Coleman's first shot.

His announcement that he was ready to party.

"Anderson!" Del cried, and there was both relief and fear in that sound. It appeased something inside me to hear how much she cared. How much the prospect of being taken away hurt her. I watched through the open window, observing the situation as the last of the Disciples filtered out of the cabin door and ducked for cover, with Cole's shots targeting them from his perch in the tree stand out front that I'd set up for emergency security situations.

Jonathan shuffled her past the window, going for the door and using her body as his shield while she fought against him. She bucked her weight, dropping to the floor suddenly and grabbing one of the shards of glass off the floor.

The angle was wrong for Cole to have a clear shot, with Jonathan hiding in the wall between the door and the window. I moved, lunging for the porch and darting across the space. Shooting a Disciple between the eyes as he made to grab me, I evaded them all and leaped in through the window. Del's hand dripped blood from where she clutched the glass shard too tightly, staring at Jonathan like she might kill him herself.

I wouldn't blame her, but the indecision on her face told me the truth I'd already known. Del would never forgive herself for taking a life.

Even his.

Drawing her into my arms, I didn't have such hesitation as I raised my Glock to take aim. His mouth trembled, words forming like he could charm his way out of the shitshow he started. Without a word for him, I fired.

The bullet caught him directly in the middle of his face,

obliterating his nose, and his body slumped back against the wall. I turned my gaze down to Del, my eyes roving over her for any injuries. There wasn't a scratch on her, despite the bruises I suspected would appear overnight. "Del," I whispered, hoping she could forgive me the deaths. Given her upbringing, and her eventual break from all she believed, I never knew where Del stood when it came to her faith.

"I guess I don't need an Annulment," she whispered, staring at what had once been the face of the man who led the only family she ever knew. There was a light-hearted joke to her tone, something I'd barely heard from her, given the stress of knowing she was hunted by a monster.

I grinned down at her, knowing more than ever that my woman was perfect.

"Anderson!" Coleman's voice echoed through the window. Snapping my head to look out, the sight of one of Jonathan's followers with an assault rifle greeted me. Fury owned his face—absolutely despair at the loss of his leader.

I twisted my body backward, tackling Del to the floor as the sound of automatic fire resounded behind me. The impact forced the breath from her lungs, but I couldn't think about that then. Not when she curled her body into me as I covered her, pinning her and protecting her with my own body.

"Anderson," she cried, running a hand over my face when the shooting stopped only a few seconds later.

"Clear!" Cole yelled. "You good?"

"We're good!" I yelled back, shoving to my feet and helping Del up. My shoulder burned, the lone bullet wound spreading fire through my veins.

"We are not good!" Del called. "Anderson's been shot!"

"Is he dead?" Coleman teased, climbing down from the perch in the tree and stepping into the light of the porch.

"It isn't funny," she whispered, turning me to examine the entry wound and the blood leaking through my shirt.

"Baby, I'm good. The team doctor is on his way already, and he'll fix me up," I murmured, touching my lips to hers softly. "Besides, now I'm symmetrical."

"I'm going to kill you," she laughed, burying her face in my chest. Only Del could make me feel at home, like everything was right in the world, when my house was destroyed and there were bodies everywhere.

Perfect.

12

DELIVERANCE

I watched Anderson's doctor friend stitch him up after he'd finished with the bullet wound. Anderson barely flinched when the man dug the bullet out, and I tried not to think about what that implied for his pain tolerance and where it came from.

The thought of him suffering and in pain was enough to bring me to my knees. Particularly after I'd thought him lost to me.

"We have to get Noelle. We can't leave her there; they might hurt her because of how she helped me escape. What if they blame her for Jonathan's death?" I asked, wincing when Anderson stood without a single hitch of pain. I'd been rendered useless by a fractured wrist, but he didn't flinch at a bullet wound.

"Tomorrow, Baby. It isn't safe to go tonight," Anderson said, but he nodded. He wore a determined expression, and I knew he would help me save her. He wouldn't leave the woman who was responsible for my own escape to suffer.

"Okay," I agreed, pressing my face into his chest and breathing him in. I wanted to surround myself with his scent, with that woodsy pine of the mountain that only he made attractive. Hammers pounded plywood into the broken window for the night as Anderson's friends made quick work of cleaning up the house as best as possible.

"You two should stay with me tonight. We don't know if they'll come back," Coleman sighed, staring at the door like he relished the thought of a house guest just as much as the pained expression on Anderson's showed how little he liked the idea.

"We'll be fine. Miguel is going to keep an eye out tonight, and then after we go to get Noelle tomorrow, we'll have a better idea where we stand with the cult. I know they won't be fond of us, but as long as they leave us alone, I couldn't give a shit," Anderson grunted.

"Noelle?"

"One of Jonathan's other wives," Anderson explained, saving me from having to. Coleman's brow furrowed in confusion, but he shrugged it off just as quickly. I had already gathered that taking more than one wife was not typical outside the *Children of Awe*. "Now, if you wouldn't mind, I'd like to go to bed."

Cole chuckled, raising his eyebrows at Anderson in a gesture that seemed meaningful. I couldn't wait for the day when I understood all the hidden meanings to their social interactions, but for that night all I wanted was to shower and curl up in bed. When Anderson sent me up ahead of him, I didn't waste a moment before stepping into the claw-foot tub and letting the hot water wash away the touch of the other men.

Of men I'd thought I'd known.

The blood on the back of my neck and in my hair stained the tub pink, reminding me of the death of a boy who'd been kind once. Before our goals opposed one another, and his blind faith in a leader who didn't deserve his loyalty had corrupted his mind against all that was right and good.

Real men of God didn't force women to stay in marriages that proved dangerous to them. I didn't know what I believed after my experiences. Only that I had time to decide for myself, and that was all that mattered to me.

When I finally stepped out of the tub and moved to the bedroom to grab a shirt and crawl under the covers, Anderson perched on the edge of the bed. His hair was wet, and I assumed he'd showered in the bathroom downstairs before coming up. "Everyone gone home?" I asked, rubbing the back of my neck nervously. The towel wrapped around my body clung to my chest tightly, but Anderson's eyes roved over me like I was already naked as he stood from the bed and prowled toward me.

"No," I scolded him, and stepped back when he reached for the towel. "You're injured."

"So are you," he grunted. "You were injured the first time I fucked you and I didn't let that stop me. What makes you think I'd let a bullet wound get in my way of being inside you?"

I chuckled, dancing away from him until rough hands grabbed the towel and tugged it away, despite my efforts to hold onto it. "You brute!" I shrieked when he wrapped his hands around my waist and lifted me onto the bed. "You'll hurt yourself."

"The only thing that hurts me is not being inside you," he grumbled, climbing up onto the bed and settling between my legs. His fingers dove between them, finding me ready for him already. "And she's already wet for me," he whispered, replacing his fingers with his cock and working himself inside without preamble.

"Anderson," I cried out, arching my back and reveling in our connection. I'd never tire of being with him. Never get over the way he made me feel.

"Could have lost you," he grunted, settling his weight over me and leaning forward to touch the tip of his nose to mine. With our faces so close, all I could see was him.

All that existed was his stare on mine and the slow roll of his hips as he took me in slow, deep thrusts.

"You didn't," I reminded him, feeling like he needed the words to remember that, no matter how close we'd come, we both walked away in the end.

The worst was over. I didn't suspect revenge would be a massive ordeal to consider.

"I love you," I told him, wrapping my hand around the back of his neck and my legs around his waist. "Don't ever let me go."

"Never Baby. You're mine now," he echoed back. His thrusts turned harsher, the slow rhythm of them lost to the need to claim me for himself. The grind of him against me and the knowledge that he was close to his own release sent me spiraling into the white, shuddering in his arms as he finished.

Unlike the first time, he separated himself from me more quickly. Staring at the space between my legs, he refused to let me close them. His fingers moved to gather up the liquid that spilled free and shove it back inside me. I thought to say something, but the intensity on his face wouldn't let me.

I had a feeling I wouldn't be getting much sleep. Considering how tired I was, that was still somehow fine with me.

∞∞∞

Anderson and Coleman's friends all joined us in our journey to the *Children of Awe* the next day. It felt strange, returning to the place that I once called home. Even looking on from the distance as we observed them in the woods, something felt different than before.

I knew it was that I'd never belonged. I'd never even wanted to.

With Anderson at my side, I had everything that mattered to me.

"You do not leave my side," he grunted, wrapping himself around my back. While there was no weapon in anyone's hand, I knew just how well armed they were beneath the surface.

"Who is that?" Coleman asked, gesturing to where a tall blond was bent over the well. She stared into the abyss, deep in thought and oblivious to the people hovering at the edge of the compound and waiting for the right moment to make themselves known.

"That's Noelle," I whispered, studying his face. Something about the way he fixated on her reminded me of the way Anderson looked at me.

"Well, shit," Anderson laughed, patting his friend on the back.

Coleman didn't wait for the others to be ready before he stalked forward into the clearing. His gait was determined and his gaze fully focused on his goal.

Noelle.

EPILOGUE
ANDERSON

*D*rinking my lemonade and taking a break from painting, I watched my wife and daughter dig their hands into the soil of the garden. Del let the dirt trickle from her closed fist, using the other hand to point out all the traits of healthy earth to Skye. She pointed to the pictures in the book resting on the ground beside them, talking about all the plants we would grow. There was a mix of talking about her own knowledge and reading the descriptions of each plant to our girl, like Del just couldn't help but read whenever she could.

Every bit her mother's daughter, Skye possessed a green thumb that appeared before she'd even started walking. At only two years old, Del and I had to force her inside at the end of the day and scrub the dirt from her body because of her enthusiasm for gardening.

Del got onto her hands and knees, maneuvering her body up to a standing position gracefully despite her growing stomach. It wouldn't be long before she had no choice but to accept my help getting up, and only a little longer before she couldn't kneel on the ground at all.

Our son would make his appearance in a few short months, much to Del's dismay. The construction on the addition of the cabin to give both Skye and Trent their own rooms had only just been completed, and with her nesting impulse kicking into full swing, she was like an impatient hellion on a mission while she waited for a day when she and Noelle could go shopping together.

"Daddy!" Skye shouted, running across the grass with her awkward gait as Del turned her grey eyes to watch. She rested her hands on her hips, showing just how much her back already started to bother her when she leaned over too much with Skye.

"You have to stop catering to her demands. She'll become a little monster," I teased her, kissing Skye's nose while she giggled.

"I can't fault her for loving the garden. It's beautiful," Del sighed, turning to look at the flourishing garden and the raised beds she'd transformed from pitiful to plentiful.

"It is," I murmured back. "I finished painting the little monster's new room finally. Thought she might like to see it."

Del moved into the house with a pout on her face. She already knew that I wouldn't let her anywhere near those paint fumes when she was pregnant with my baby. She moved to the nursery instead, staring at the moss green walls in consideration since she could finally be in the room and plan out her nesting frenzy.

Skye and I left her to it, walking to the room across the hall. With the windows thrown wide open, the smell wasn't too horrible, but I wouldn't take any chances. The sunny yellow paint on the walls had been Skye's choice, matching her cheerful personality with her favorite color.

My daughter would never know what it was to be

controlled the way her mother had. She'd never have to worry about men dictating her life.

I'd kill any who tried.

"'Lellow!" Skye cheered, bouncing up and down happily. "Mommy, Lellow!" she called, making Del chuckle in the other room.

Everything was sunshine for my girls, and I'd make sure it stayed that way.

I hope you enjoyed Deliverance & Anderson's story! Please consider taking the time to leave me a review. Hearing from my readers means the world to me. Keep an eye out for news of Noelle & Coleman's story. Coming soon.

If you loved Anderson and his possessive nature, consider taking a walk on the dark side with Bloodied Hands. The mafia men of my Bellandi Crime Syndicate take possessive to another level.

>>>Download Bloodied Hands

*V*isit my website to find out more or sign up for my mailing list to receive the latest updates.

>>>www.AdelaideForrest.com

ALSO BY ADELAIDE FORREST

BELLANDI WORLD SYNDICATE UNIVERSE

Bellandi Crime Syndicate Series

Bloodied Hands

Forgivable Sins

Grieved Loss

Shielded Wrongs

Scarred Regrets

Beauty in Lies Series

Until Tomorrow Comes

Until Forever Ends

Until Retribution Burns

Until Death Do Us Part

OTHER DARK ROMANCE

An Initiation of Thorns - Cowritten with Tove Madigan

Pawn of Lies

ROMANTIC SUSPENSE NOVELLAS

The Men of Mount Awe Series

Deliver Me from Evil

Kings of Conquest - Cowritten with Lyric Cox

Claiming His Princess

Stealing His Princess

Printed in Great Britain
by Amazon

82824624R00051